The Egg

Written by Jill Eggleton
Illustrated by Mary Ann Hurley

Rigby

Charlie Cook and I went
to Baboon Beach on the island
of Sambuska. We were digging
holes in the sand when we dug up
an enormous egg. We had never
seen an egg like it! It looked
really old. We knew we had made
a very **IMPORTANT** discovery.

The Island of Sambuska

We put the egg in our beach towels to keep it safe and then went to the library.

We found out that our egg was the egg of the giant elephant bird! It was over . . .

two thousand years old!

Elephant Birds were like ostriches, only much bigger and much heavier. People say these birds were more than six feet high and weighed as much as a small elephant! They have been extinct for over 2,000 years.

We couldn't figure out how the egg had gotten to Sambuska Island. We thought it had been carried there by the sea. The egg must have been buried deep in the sand for years and years.

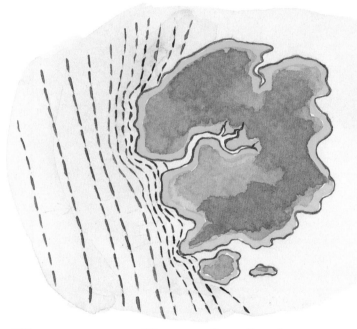

We were really excited about our egg. We took it home and made a special box for it. We hoped that the egg would make us famous, and it did!

7

The news about our egg was on radio and television.

A rich man wanted to give us

$500,000.00 for the egg!

He thought the egg would make him a lot of money.

But Mr. Floss, who looked after Baboon Beach, was angry that Charlie and I had taken the egg. He said that it was wrong to dig it up.

He said that the egg should stay buried on Baboon Beach on Sambuska Island.

Wow

Charlie and I were
really upset.

We didn't know what to do
with the egg. We couldn't leave
it anywhere. We felt bad about
digging it up.

So we went back to Baboon
Beach and buried the egg again.

Now only Charlie and I knew
where the elephant bird's egg
was buried. We had a secret.

We hoped that the egg would
stay buried for another two
thousand years.

The people of Sambuska Island were very upset with Mr. Floss. They said that Charlie and I had looked after the egg. They said we should get a reward for finding it.

The people said it was . . .

an amazing egg!

Charlie and I knew that it would not be right for us to keep the egg a secret.

We said we would dig the egg up again.

13

The people of Sambuska Island gave us a reward for finding the egg. The egg was taken to the museum.

This certificate was given to

Jim Brown
and
Charlie Cook

for finding the Elephant Bird's Egg and giving it to the Sambuska Museum

Elephant Bird's Egg

Now Sambuska Island is a famous place. People come from all over the world. They come to see the gigantic elephant bird's egg. They look at the egg and they wonder how it came across the ocean to Baboon Beach. They wonder how it had stayed buried in the sand for all those years. They read the words on the gold plate by the egg . . .

Elephant Bird's Egg reckoned to be over 2,000 years old. Found by Jim Brown and Charlie Cook on Baboon Beach, Sambuska Island.

Elephant Bird's
Egg

17

Recounts

Recounts tell about something that has happened.

A recount tells the reader

- what happened

- to whom

- where it happened

- when it happened

A recount has events in sequence . . .

. . . and a
conclusion

Guide Notes

> **Title: The Egg Saga**
> **Stage:** Fluency (1)
>
> **Text Form:** Recount
> **Approach:** Guided Reading
> **Processes:** Thinking Critically, Exploring Language, Processing Information
> **Written and Visual Focus**: Recount Structure, Text Highlights, Certificate,
> Speech Bubbles

THINKING CRITICALLY
(sample questions)
- Why do you think the egg had never been discovered before?
- How do you think the egg could have gotten to Sambuska Island?
- What might you have done if you had found an egg like that?
- Why do you think it would not have been right to keep the egg a secret?
- How do you think Sambuska Island might have changed because of the egg?

EXPLORING LANGUAGE

Terminology
Spread, author and illustrator credits, ISBN number

Vocabulary
Clarify: saga, discovery, extinct, amazing, famous
Nouns: egg, sand, museum, library, box
Verbs: dig, bury, look
Singular/plural: egg/eggs, beach/beaches, person/people

Print Conventions
Apostrophes – possessive (elephant bird's egg), contraction (couldn't)

Phonological Patterns
Focus on short and long vowel **o** (**o**ld, **o**strich, g**o**t, h**o**ped, **o**ver)
Discuss root words – buried, digging, heavier, carried
Discuss the silent letter in – **w**rong, **k**new